FATHER TO SON II
KAIDEN FACES HIS FEARS

WRITTEN BY: KENJI L. JACKSON

WITH: HEDDRICK MCBRIDE

ILLUSTRATED BY: HH-PAX

EDITED BY: JILL MCKELLAN

ENJOY !

2017

Dedication

This book is dedicated to all the children who do not let their fears get the best of them, and the parents who support their children and assist them in overcoming their fears. The inspiration behind the Father to Son series comes from my son Kaiden Li. He motivates me to strive to be a better man and the best father possible. I'd like to thank my parents, family, closest friends, the men of TTC, and my Morgan State University Alumni family for their continued love and support.

Kaiden Gets a Haircut

It's a wonderful Saturday morning
with blue skies and sunshine.
Dad is taking Kaiden to the barbershop
for the very first time.

After a short wait the time has come to sit
in the barber's chair.

The owner, Mr. Shakoor,
is going to cut Kaiden's hair.

Kaiden takes a seat
and Mr. Shakoor is ready to start.
He turns on the clippers
and things quickly fall apart.

Kaiden grows very afraid
and suddenly begins to cry.
His dad is right by his side
and thinks he knows why.

Dad asks, "What's wrong, son?"
as Kaiden's tears wet his shirt.
Kaiden says, "That thing is noisy
and I know it is going to hurt!"

Mr. Shakoor replies, "These clippers won't hurt
and don't worry about the noise.
The sounds let me know the clippers work,
just like sounds do with your toys."

Mr. Shakoor hands Kaiden
the clippers to hold and feel.
Kaiden calms down and happily says,
"These clippers are no big deal."

Dad pats Kaiden on the back
and Kaiden sits big and tall.
Mr. Shakoor continues cutting his hair
and it doesn't hurt even a little, not at all.

Kaiden's haircut is finally finished,
no pain and no worries.
He climbs out of the chair and heads
to the mirror in a hurry.

Kaiden is all smiles and excitedly thanks
his dad and Mr. Shakoor.
He really likes his new haircut
and isn't afraid anymore!

Kaiden goes to a New School

school

After only one year at his school,
Kaiden is in for a big change.
His family is moving to an area
out of his school's range.

Kaiden likes his teachers, the principal,
and has made lots of friends.
Now that he is moving,
Kaiden will have to start all over again.

Kaiden is sad and angry,
not sure what he should think or do.
His dad understands
because he is nervous about moving, too.

The truck is packed and ready to go.
Today is the day.
Kaiden and his family get in the truck
and head to a town far away.

During the drive Kaiden is looking out the window
and hasn't said a word.
Dad says, "Son, your new teacher
and classmates are nice, that's what I've heard."

"How am I going to make new friends?" Kaiden asks.
His face is draped with a frown.
Dad exclaims, "I'm sure there are plenty of cool kids
at school and around town."

The day has finally arrived;
the first day of school is here.
Kaiden's dad takes him to his class;
easing his worries so he can face his fear.

The teacher, Mrs. Wilson, introduces him
and the students shout, "Welcome to our class!"
Kaiden says hello to everyone
but he is nervous and just wants the day to pass.

Dad hugs Kaiden and wishes him good luck
as he takes a seat to begin his day.
Mrs. Wilson checks on him from time to time
to make sure he is okay.

When lunch comes Kaiden sits by himself
listening to music because the cafeteria is very loud.
Then some of his classmates join him at his table
to make him feel like part of the crowd.

Kaiden's first day is finally over
and he feels much better about his new school.
He can't wait to tell his parents that his teacher
is awesome and his classmates are cool.

Dad knows every day will not be perfect
but having a great first day is a start.
Kaiden is excited about his classmates
and learning, too, so he can be smart.

Kaiden gets on an Airplane

It is finally that time of year
and everyone is filled with anticipation.
Dad is taking Kaiden and the family
on a summer vacation.

They are flying to Florida and summer is here,
it's the perfect season.
Everyone is excited but Kaiden
and for a very good reason.

Kaiden sadly asks, "Why can't we drive the car
instead or take the train?"
Dad replies, "Son, It is so much cooler
and faster if we fly by plane."

Dad helps Kaiden finish packing his suitcase
but all Kaiden does is worry.
Mom shouts, "Come down stairs with your bags.
We are late. We have to hurry!"

During the drive to the airport,
Dad tries to make Kaiden feel better.
Dad says, "Don't worry Kaiden,
the flight will be fun and we will all sit together."

Kaiden and his family park at the airport,
check in, board the plane, and take their seats.
Ms. Lopez, the flight attendant, greets Kaiden
with a smile and gives him a treat.

By the look of worry on Kaiden's face,
Ms. Lopez knows exactly what to say.
She exclaims, "The first time I flew
I was very afraid but now I love flying every day!"

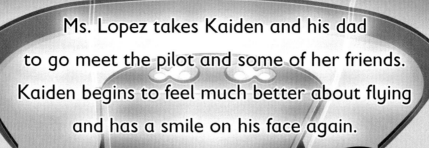

Ms. Lopez takes Kaiden and his dad
to go meet the pilot and some of her friends.
Kaiden begins to feel much better about flying
and has a smile on his face again.

All of the passengers are buckled in
and it's time for the plane to take to the sky.
Kaiden feels a huge tickle in his tummy
as the plane takes off and begins to fly.

Now the plane is coasting smoothly
as it passes through a few big clouds.
Kaiden is happily looking out the window
and his family feels proud.

After hours of flying, Kaiden's fears
are erased and the plane successfully lands.
Kaiden hugs Ms. Lopez and begins telling
her about all of his plans.

Dad thanks Ms. Lopez for helping
and gives a high five to his awesome son.
Kaiden showed he was brave
and now he thinks flying is fun.

Kaiden Goes Swimming

The summer is almost over
and a day of family fun is finally here.
Uncle Dwight is having a BIG pool party,
which he hosts every year.

Kaiden loves to dance and play
and thinks the fireworks are cool.
However, he is definitely not looking forward
to getting in the pool.

Last year Kaiden dipped his feet in
but was too afraid to get in and join the fun.
This time Kaiden wants to try to swim
even though it is something he has never done.

While walking to the party, Kaiden tells his dad
that he didn't have much fun last year.
Dad says, "I will not let anything happen to you,
son, so you have nothing to fear."

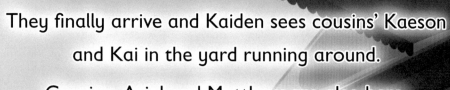

They finally arrive and Kaiden sees cousins' Kaeson
and Kai in the yard running around.

Cousins, Ariel and Matthew are also here.
They came from out of town.

After a game of tag and dancing,
the kids get into the pool to swim and play.
Ariel asks Kaiden, "Are you getting into the pool
to have some fun with us today?"

Kaiden replies nervously, "I don't know
how to swim but I am going to try."
Dad says, "Stay away from the deep end
and put this life jacket on. You will be fine."

With his dad by his side, Kaiden enters
the pool and the other kids begin cheering him on.
The water is cold but Kaiden is determined
to have fun and make sure his fear is gone.

Kaiden is wearing a life jacket which helps him
stay safely above water and swim.
Dad is excited and anxious to show Kaiden
how to swim the way his dad taught him.

Kaiden nervously lies across Dad's arms
and Dad shouts, "Kaiden kick your feet!"
With a little bit of help from his Dad,
Kaiden is swimming and exclaims, "This is neat!"

The rest of the day Kaiden and his cousins play
in the pool and eat lots of great food.
There are no more worries for Kaiden.
He's in a fantastic mood!

Dad is proud of his son and Kaiden
cannot wait until the pool party next year.
Kaiden even wants to take swimming lessons
so he can be a great swimmer without any fear!

Kaiden Has a Bad Dream

It is one o'clock in the morning and Kaiden
is tossing and turning in his sleep.
He is having a really bad dream
and suddenly wakes up and begins to weep.

It's quiet but Kaiden thinks there's a
hungry monster in his closet looking to be fed.
He quickly runs down the hallway
into his big sister's room and jumps on her bed.

"Alexia, get up, get up!" Kaiden franticly whispers
as he pushes and shoves her.

Alexia awakens confused and says,
"Get out of my room and go to sleep, little brother!"

Kaiden says, "There is a hungry monster in my closet!
Can I sleep by you?"

Looking surprised, Alexia says,
"A monster in your closet? That isn't true!"

Alexia gets out of bed, taking Kaiden by the hand
and they go down the hall.

She walks with Kaiden into his room
to help him face his fears once and for all.

As Alexia walks boldly towards the closet
Kaiden nervously follows behind.
Alexia opens the closet door and says,
"See Kaiden! No monsters of any kind!"

"You must have dreamt about them
and woke up, thinking they were real."
Alexia continues, "I used to have bad dreams, too,
so I know exactly how you feel!"

After thanking his sister for her help,
Kaiden gives her a hug and squeezes her tight.
Kaiden knows his room is safe
and gets in the bed and turns off the light.

The next morning on the way to school,
Kaiden tells his Dad all about last night.
Kaiden says, "I had a bad dream and was scared
but Alexia made everything all right!"

Kaiden feels better about sleeping in his room
and knows monsters are not real.
Kaiden now goes to sleep with no fears
and Dad thinks that is a pretty big deal!

VISIT
WWW.MCBRIDESTORIES.COM
FOR MORE TITLES

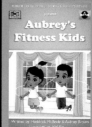